Steve McGarry

VERY FIRST

BADLANDS

ANNUAL

from

THE Sun

©1994
News Group Newspapers Ltd.

Published by

Pedigree BOOKS

Pedigree Books Limited,
The Old Rectory,
Matford Lane, Exeter,
Devon, EX2 4PS.

ISBN 1-874507-38-4
Printed in Italy

£3.99

BL1

CW00410956

MARSHAL MASK　　　**PONGO**

BADLANDS

by STEVE McGARRY

BELLE BOTTOM   **WILDERNESS WILLIE**   **SIR CRISPIN DRY**

10 THINGS YOU NEVER KNEW ABOUT

Marshal Mask isn't the only one who likes dressing up – the McGarry clan at a Cartoonist's awards dinner in America

1 Steve McGarry was born in Wythenshawe, Manchester in 1953 and attended St. Bede's Grammar School. He left school at 16 with two GCE 'O' levels.

2 He quit his art studio job in 1977 to try his luck as a full-time freelancer. His first published works were illustrations for love stories in the now-defunct girl's comic "Romeo."

3 In the late '70s, Steve designed (badly, he cheerfully confesses) record sleeves for a host of Mancunian rock luminaries – including Joy Division, Jilted John, Slaughter & The Dogs, John Cooper Clarke and the fabulously-named Ed Banger and The Nosebleeds.

4 He was once a partner in a commercial production company and sang on tv and radio ads for everything from Timpson's Shoes to Popnut Crunch popcorn.

5 Steve's pop career spluttered to a grinding halt on the Northern cabaret circuit – but among the members of Steve McGarry's First Offence who progressed a little further were Toby Toman of Primal Scream and Donald Johnson of A Certain Ratio.

6 As none of these ventures ever made any money, Steve was fortunate enough to have girlfriend Debbie in regular, gainful employment. They met in 1977 and married in 1984. Twins Joe and Luke were born in 1987.

7 Steve's cartooning career began to take off in the early '80s. His work has appeared in most British papers and dozens of magazines.

8 Badlands was launched in 1988 in Eddie Shah's ill-fated paper, The Post. When The Post folded, the strip was snapped up by Britain's biggest daily, The Sun, where it debuted in May, 1989.

9 Steve's cartoons are syndicated throughout the world by United Features in New York. His Pop Culture strip appears in Today in Britain and is syndicated to some 600 newspapers in the U.S.

10 The McGarrys have lived in America – in Huntington Beach, California – since 1989.

BOOKS AVAILABLE FROM PEDIGREE

The Gambols Annual
Take a light hearted look at married life through the daily mishaps of George and Gay Gambol, Britains most celebrated spouses. £3.99

The Beau Peep Annual
More fun and frolics in the hapless adventures of Beau Peep, featuring 96 pages of this year's funniest cartoons. £3.99

Giles Facsimile D-Day Edition
A special limited commemorative edition for D'Day, this faithfully reproduces the first ever 1946 collection of Giles Cartoons to recapture the humour of a nation at war. £14.95

The Rupert Reproduction
This authentic limited edition reproduction of the 1942 Rupert Book is as true to the original as possible right down to its soft cover. Preserved in its own slip-over case, it's destined to become as treasured and collected as the 1942 edition itself. £17.95

The Action Man Adventure Annual
Our most exciting Annual ever. 20 fun packed pages of interactive comic strip action and adventure, with built-in sound effects to make every story explode into life, plus pull-out games and masks to let young Action Men create their own adventure stories. £11.99

The 1995 Rupert Annual
Rupert bear and his friends return again in probably the world's most sought after and collected annual. £4.95

Giles Classic Cartoons
Capture the timeless wit and charm of Britain's most prolific and well loved cartoonist, with this unique collection of Giles Cartoons £3.99